Copyright © 2003 by Nord-Süd Verlag AG, Gossau Zürich, Switzerland
First published in Switzerland under the title *Der falsche Freund*.
English translation copyright © 2003 by North-South Books Inc., New York

First published in the United States, Great Britain, Canada,
Australia, and New Zealand in 2003 by North-South Books,
an imprint of Nord-Süd Verlag AG, Gossau Zürich, Switzerland.

Distributed in the United States by North-South Books Inc., New York.

Library of Congress Cataloging-in-Publication Data is available.
A CIP catalogue record for this book is available from The British Library.
ISBN 0-7358-1785-5 (trade edition) 10 9 8 7 6 5 4 3 2 1
ISBN 0-7358-1786-3 (library edition) 10 9 8 7 6 5 4 3 2 1
Printed in Belgium

For more information about our books, and the authors and artists
who create them, visit our web site: www.northsouth.com

FAIR-WEATHER FRIEND

by **Udo Weigelt**

Illustrated by **Nora Hilb**

Translated by J. Alison James

North-South Books
New York / London

FINN was a big red cat whose best friend was a hamster named Max. Their family had just moved to a new house. Finn and Max were enjoying the sunshine on the front steps when they heard a loud *meow!*

It was a gang of cats.

They looked tough. They looked brave. They looked adventurous. Finn's eyes opened wide.

"You're new, aren't you," mewed the striped cat. "I'm Number One, and this here is my gang—Number Two, Number Three, and Number Four. Who are you?"

"My name is Finn," said Finn. "I'm pleased to meet you."

"We don't use real names around here," Number One said with a quiet growl. "We keep them secret."

Finn felt a thrill. He wanted to change his name and stalk the alleyways with these dangerous cats.

Then Number Three looked straight at Max the hamster and snarled, "Nice catch. If you want to join our gang, you'll have to share. We share everything."

Finn was horrified.

"This is no 'catch'—he's Max, my best friend," said Finn. Max smiled and waved to the cats.

"Nonsense!" said Number Two. "Cats aren't friends with hamsters. Cats *eat* hamsters."

"Never!" cried Finn.

The cats hissed furiously. Max cowered under his friend. For a moment it seemed as if the gang was going to pounce on them both.

Then Number One said, "Well, if you insist, we won't eat that juicy little hamster. But if you stay friends with him, you can forget being part of our gang. We'll give you until tomorrow to decide. Think about it."

Then the cats walked away, their tails swishing in the air.

Max ran back in the house to safety. Finn came after, dragging his tail. He didn't feel like playing. He curled up with his eyes closed so Max would leave him alone.

Why couldn't a cat be friends with a hamster, he wondered.

Max tried to cheer Finn up. He put on his wizard's costume and did a little dance. He even tickled Finn behind the ears. But nothing worked. Finn was still sad.

"I've got an idea," Max said at last. "What if you pretend that we *aren't* friends. You can play with those mean scary cats when you are outside, and inside we can play together like always."

Finn sat up. "That's a great idea," he said.

The next morning the gang of cats arrived. Finn said good-bye to Max and went outside.

"Good, you came to your senses," said Number One. "From now on we'll call you Number Five."

Finn was proud of his new name. He whisked his tail high. Then he looked back over his shoulder and saw Max sitting alone in the window, and he felt sad.

But he couldn't think of a better solution. So in the mornings, Number Five roamed with the gang and missed Max. In the afternoons, Finn played inside and missed the cats. He was busy, but he wasn't really happy.

Then one day when Max thought Finn and the gang were far away he went outside by himself. Suddenly he heard a strange howling gasp. Max ran to see what was wrong. There was Number One, with her collar snagged on a fence. She was having a hard time breathing.

"Hold on, I'll help you!" cried Max. He jumped up and started chewing through her collar as fast as he could. Soon the collar broke away, and Number One could breathe again.

"Oh my!" gasped Number One. "That was a close one. Thank you!"

Just then Finn came around the corner with the gang. Finn saw Max standing there, just inches from Number One's sharp claws. "Leave him alone," Finn yowled. "Don't you dare eat Max!"

"You'd better watch what you say to Number One," said Number Two threateningly. "She'll kick you out of the gang!"

"I don't care if she does!" said Finn.

"Don't worry," said Number One, "this little guy is my friend now!" Number One told the rest of the gang how Max had saved her life.

And that was how Max got to join the gang. They called him Number Five-and-a-half, and they took turns carrying him on their backs all over town.